Snow White and the Seven Dwarfs

I do not make films primarily for children. I make them for the child in all of us, whether we be six or sixty. Call the child innocence. The worst of us is not without innocence, although buried deeply it might be. In my work I try to reach and speak to that innocence, showing it the fun and joy of living; showing it that laughter is healthy; showing it that the human species, although happily ridiculous at times, is still reaching for the stars.

*Our gratitude for their cooperation and generous assistance
to all the people of Walt Disney Productions, but particularly
Vince Jefferds, Don MacLaughlin, Wayne Morris, Tom Golberg and Jeanette Kroger.*

Originally published in a Limited Edition in 1978
by Circle Fine Art Press

Published in 1979, with additional text, by The Viking Press,
625 Madison Avenue, New York, N.Y. 10022

Published simultaneously in Canada by
Penguin Books Canada Limited

Executive Editor: Jack Solomon, Jr.
Production and Art Director: Marshall Lee
Design: Frank Rowland and Marshall Lee

Library of Congress Cataloging in Publication Data
Snow White and the seven dwarfs.

   Walt Disney's Snow White and the seven dwarfs.
   (A Studio book)
   Summary: More than 400 of the original drawings,
sketches, and paintings used in preparing the 1937
film, together with the classic tale, present a history
of the creation of Disney's first full-length animated
feature.
   1. Snow White and the seven dwarfs.   [Motion picture]
   2. Moving-picture cartoons, American.
[1. Snow White and the seven dwarfs.   [Motion picture]
   2. Animation (Cinematography)   3. Fairy tales]
I. Disney (Walt) Productions.   II. Title.
NC1766.U53S64   398.2   79-14892
ISBN 0-670-65381-0

Printed in the United States of America

CONTENTS

Snow White and the Seven Dwarfs

 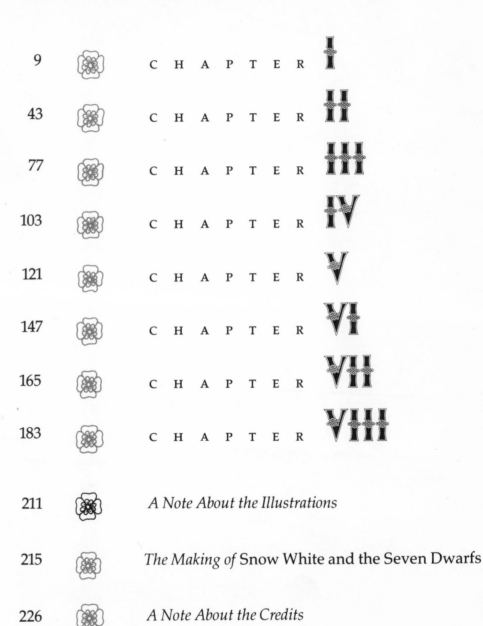

nce upon a time, there lived a lovely little Princess named Snow White. Her vain and wicked stepmother, the Queen, feared that someday Snow White's beauty would surpass her own. So she dressed the little Princess in rags and forced her to work as a scullery maid.

Each day the evil Queen consulted her Magic Mirror. "Magic Mirror on the wall," she would chant. "Who is the fairest one of all?"

And as long as the Mirror answered, "You are the fairest one of all," Snow White was safe from the Queen's cruel jealousy.

In spite of the way the Queen treated her, Snow White was happy, and often sang as she went about her humble tasks. One day she was busily scrubbing the steps in the courtyard of the castle, humming softly to herself. When she noticed that her pail was nearly empty, the Princess rose from her hands and knees and went to the well to draw more water.

"I'll tell you a secret," she confided to the birds perched on the well. "This is a Wishing Well. I'm going to make a wish into the well, and if it echoes back, my wish will come true."

With that, Snow White leaned down to make her wish.

As her words began to echo back from the well, there was a wild flutter of wings as the birds started up in alarm. The Princess smiled gently. Like every young girl, she was wishing for her true love.

So intent on her wish was Snow White that she didn't hear the lone rider approaching the castle. Surely, here was her wish come true—a handsome Prince on a white horse.

The Prince dismounted and approached Snow White. Realizing she was no longer alone, the Princess spun around in surprise, a look of alarm on her face.

"Oh!' gasped the lovely Princess. "You frightened me!"

The Prince was about to apologize for alarming her, but Snow White, like a startled deer, turned and fled back into the castle.

"Wait!" cried the Prince. "Please don't run away!"

But Snow White wouldn't stop until she'd gained the safety of the castle balcony. There she finally stopped, and turned to look down at the stranger. Certainly, he was handsome. Then the Prince smiled up at her, and she knew from the kind light in his eyes that she had nothing to fear from him.

"Now that I've found you," he called, "I must know your name. I've searched everywhere for you."

The Princess Snow White blushed and waved to him shyly, then went indoors.

Her stepmother, the Queen, meanwhile, was in a fury. She had again consulted her Magic Mirror, and this time it had given her the answer she feared most: "Snow White is the fairest one of all!"

Sitting on her throne in an icy rage, she summoned her huntsman. He came before her, hat in hand, making an effort not to seem afraid.

"You will take the Princess Snow White out into the forest," the Queen snarled. "Pick a secluded spot, and there, my faithful huntsman," she continued, "you will kill her!"

"But . . . Your Majesty . . ." protested the huntsman.

"Silence!" snapped the Queen. "You know the penalty if you fail me! But to make sure you obey me," she purred, with an evil smile, "bring me her heart in this!" And she thrust a small box into his hands.

"Yes, Your Majesty." The huntsman bowed, went to find Snow White, and took her into the forest.

Snow White was enjoying her forest outing. As she stooped to gather flowers, she spied a baby bird that had fallen from its nest. Tenderly she picked up the fledgling.

"Why, where are your mama and papa?" she asked. The Princess was occupied with the chick, and hadn't seen the huntsman draw his knife and raise it above her, ready to strike.

Suddenly, some sixth sense warned Snow White of danger. She whirled around and saw the huntsman's knife.

Snow White screamed and
shrank back against a rock.

The huntsman, remorseful, dropped
his knife and sank to his knees.
"Forgive me, Your Highness," he
sobbed. "The Queen commanded me to
kill you, but I cannot do it."

Snow White gasped.

"She is mad," he explained, "jealous of your beauty. She'll stop at nothing to destroy you. You must run away, child, hide somewhere! Never return!"

Snow White was stunned, and plunged blindly into the forest. It was a dark place, echoing with the sounds of owls and other forest creatures. Each tree seemed to clutch at her as she ran, and she fancied she saw grotesque faces and glowing eyes in the gloom. Finally the Princess collapsed on the ground, terrified and exhausted, unable to run any farther.

Now the eyes glowing in a ring around her came closer and closer.

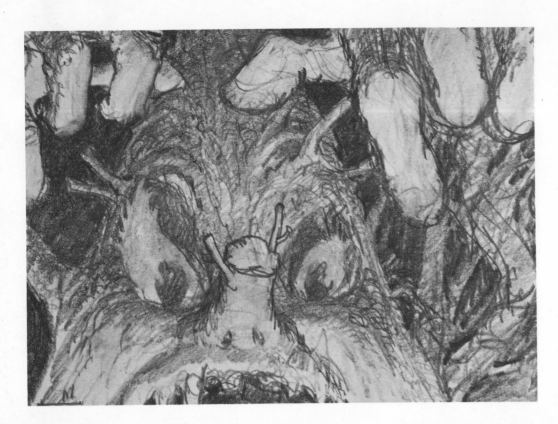

Snow White sobbed brokenly. Then, all at once, the glowing orbs resolved into the eyes of rabbits, squirrels, a fawn, and other forest creatures.

"Oh!" said the Princess, sitting up. The startled animals hastily backed away from her. "Please don't run away," she entreated. "I didn't mean to frighten you."

The smaller animals, sensing her gentleness, slowly crept up to her. And Snow White began to realize that what had seemed ill fortune was, in fact, good luck—she was away from the castle and out of reach of her wicked stepmother, the Queen.

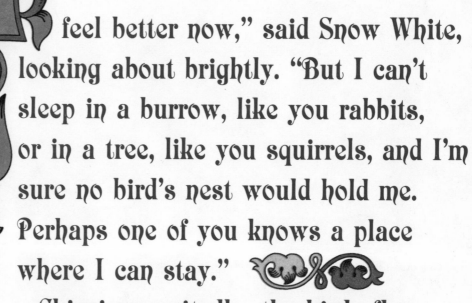

I feel better now," said Snow White, looking about brightly. "But I can't sleep in a burrow, like you rabbits, or in a tree, like you squirrels, and I'm sure no bird's nest would hold me. Perhaps one of you knows a place where I can stay."

Chirping excitedly, the birds flew down, took hold of her cape, and began to lead the Princess off through the woods. Before long, they came to a large clearing. Snow White stopped to gaze in amazement at the scene that lay before her. Here in the middle of the dense forest was a small meadow with a stream running through it.

"—OR IN A TREE THE
WAY YOU DO—

"I CAN'T SLEEP IN THE GRO
LIKE YOU—

On the far side of the clearing stood a small, snug cottage. A ray of sunshine beamed down on it, making its thatched straw roof gleam like gold.

To Snow White, the cottage in the clearing looked like just the haven she needed.

"What a perfect little house," she said, and started toward it. The little Princess and the animals peered in the windows. Snow White rubbed at a pane of glass to get a clearer view.

"Ooh!" she murmured. "It's dark inside." She knocked on the door, but there was no answer. Gathering her courage, Snow White opened the door and went inside.

"Hello! Anybody home?" she called. Again there was no answer. The animals followed her inside.

"Oh!" cried Snow White in delight. "What a cute little chair! Why, there are seven little chairs and seven places at the table!"

But the Princess noticed, as she looked around the room, that whoever the occupants of the little cottage were, they were very untidy. Scattered all over the room were piles of clothing, dirty dishes, and tools. Every surface was coated with dust and cobwebs.

Snow White's forest friends gazed in dismay at the confusion, shaking their heads. The Princess shook her head, too. "This room has never been swept," she scolded. "What untidy children! You'd think their mother and father would . . ." She paused as a thought struck her. "Maybe they have no parents. Maybe they're orphans . . ."

Snow White was already feeling sorry for the seven little orphans she'd never seen. She turned to the animals, a determined expression on her face.

"These poor children! No parents—no one to clean and cook for them, no one to bake them cookies and pies . . ."

"Well, we'll take care of that," she declared. "We're going to clean house for them and surprise them when they get back. Then, maybe," she finished thoughtfully, "they'll let me stay here."

The Princess and her animal friends all fell to with a will. After taking off her cape, Snow White assigned the tasks. The squirrels began to wash the dishes, while the bunnies and chipmunks started on the sooty fireplace.

Snow White herself began to sweep the room. She sang a merry tune, and the animals worked in time with her melody.

The deer dusted, chipmunks and squirrels helped the fawn with the dishes, while yet another chipmunk began to brush away the cobwebs from the rafters. Outside the cottage the raccoons were washing clothes in the brook, draping the wet garments over a deer's antlers to dry.

Several of the birds found flowers, and placed them, one by one, in the vase in the middle of the table, putting the finishing touch on a room that was by now spotless, ready for the return of the "orphans."

"Oh, thank you all so much!" said the grateful Princess.

HANGS
THEN HAT ON
OVER — THEN TH
OF CLOTHES ON HEAD
OUT TO LEFT — SQUIRREL
PANTS ARE COMING

Not far away from the activity in the cottage was a diamond mine. Seven little men there were stowing away the results of the day's work and preparing to go home. None of them was more than three feet tall, but what they lacked in size they made up in energy.

One of the dwarfs bent to squint at a glittering object in the path of the ore-cart. He picked it up, examined it carefully, then discarded it as the clock chimed five. Since it was time to close up the mine and return home, the seven dwarfs shouldered their pickaxes and began the homeward march in single file, singing merrily as they went.

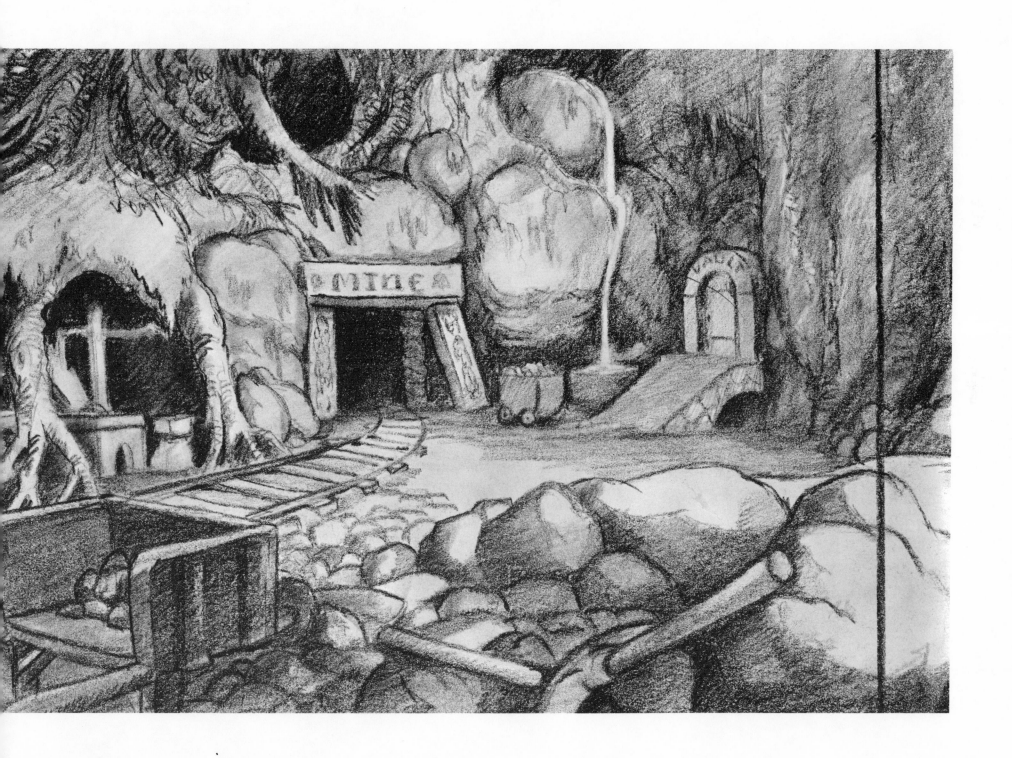

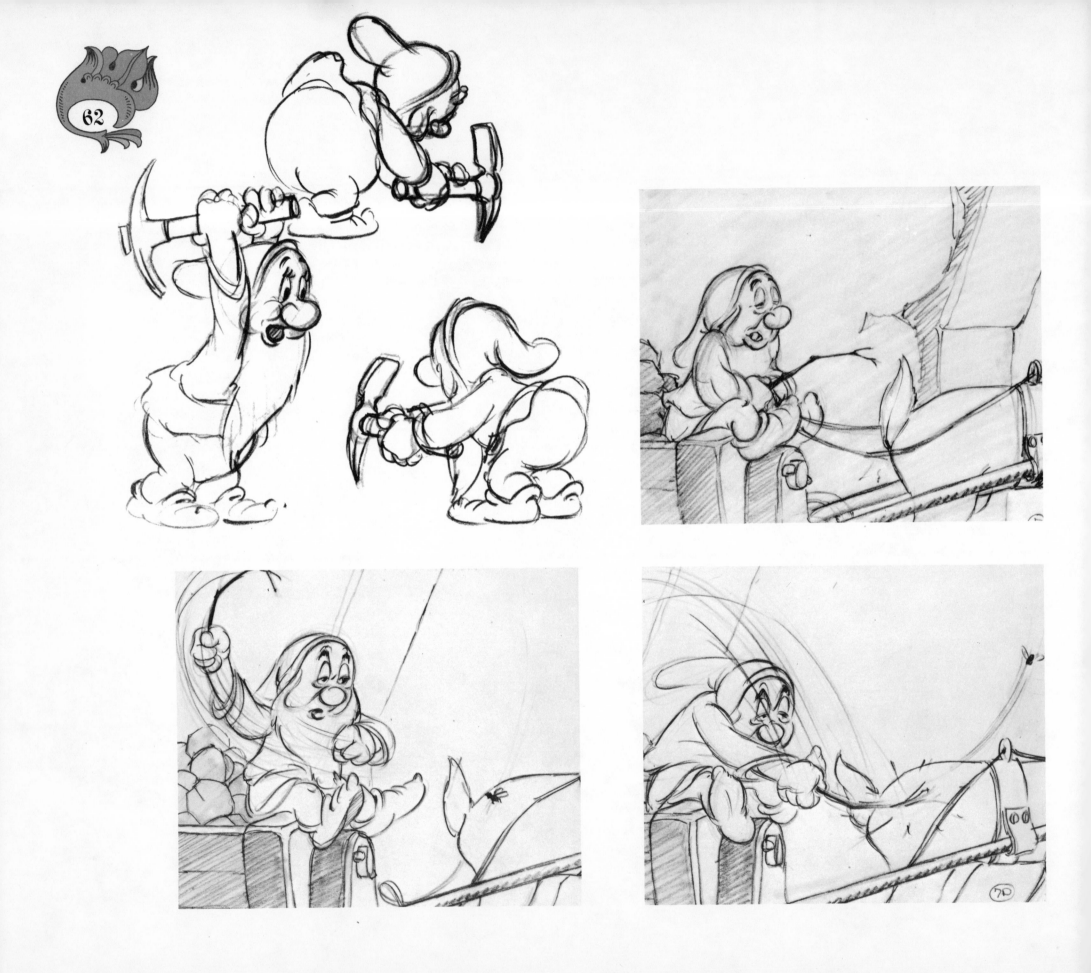

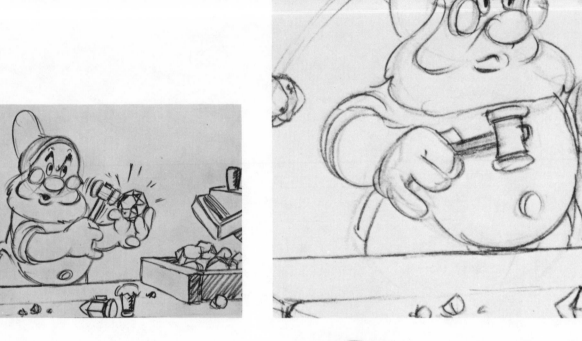

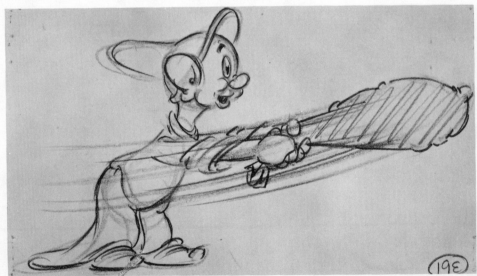

Meanwhile, back in the cottage, the cleaning operation had finally been completed to Snow White's satisfaction. She stood back and surveyed their handiwork with pride.

"There," she breathed. "Doesn't that look better now?" Then she looked around and found a candle and lit it, for the evening shadows were lengthening. "Now let's see what's upstairs," she beckoned.

At the top of the stairs was a door. Snow White opened it, and they all trooped inside, pausing to stare at the seven little beds neatly arranged in rows against the walls.

"Why, what adorable beds!" exclaimed Snow White, holding up the candle. "And look—the children's names are carved on them!"

The Princess peered closer. "Doc … Happy … Sneezy … Dopey … Grumpy … Bashful …" she read slowly, "and Sleepy. What odd names for children!" Then she yawned, all at once realizing how tired she was.

"I'm a little sleepy, myself," she said. "I'll just take a nap…" The exhausted Princess stretched herself across three beds and fell fast asleep. The birds picked up a blanket and draped it across her.

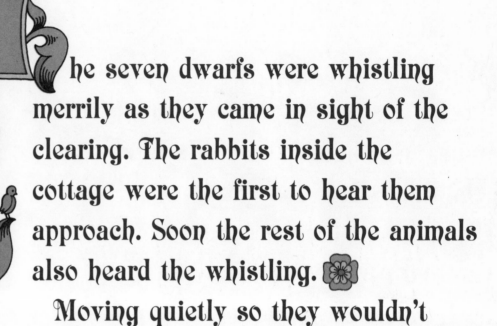

The seven dwarfs were whistling merrily as they came in sight of the clearing. The rabbits inside the cottage were the first to hear them approach. Soon the rest of the animals also heard the whistling.

Moving quietly so they wouldn't wake the sleeping Princess, the forest creatures crept downstairs and out of the cottage. They quickly disappeared into the woods.

The dwarfs marched into the clearing in single file. Doc, in the lead, stopped abruptly, and the others piled into him. The whistling died and the dwarfs stared at their cottage in silence.

"What's the matter?" asked Sneezy.

"Look!" Doc's finger pointed at their cottage. "Our house…the lit's light, er, the light's lit!"

The seven little men scattered for cover, and peered cautiously at their home. Someone was definitely inside!

"Door's open!"

"Chimney's smokin'!"

"Somebody's in there!"

Suggestions were made—a goblin, a demon, or even a dragon. Finally Grumpy spoke up. "There's trouble brewin'—mark my words!"

"What'll we do?" the others asked in apprehension.

"Let's sneak up on it," suggested Happy, as he moved to the rear.

"That's it!" agreed Doc. "We'll squeak up, er, sneak up. Follow me!"

Carefully the seven dwarfs crept up to the cottage, ready to turn and run at the slightest sign of movement. But nothing stirred, and they reached the windows and peered in. Then Doc opened the door and they went inside.

At first all they could do was stare in amazement at how neat and clean the cottage was. Then Doc spoke.

"Careful, men," he warned. "Search every cook 'n nanny, uh, hook 'n granny, uh…oh, search everywhere."

The dwarfs began to search the cottage. "Look," said Doc. "The floor's been swept." 🌸

"Huh! The chair's been dusted," mumbled Grumpy.

"Gosh, our cobwebs are missin'," noticed Bashful, peering up at the sparkling clean rafters.

"Why, the whole place is clean," said Doc.

"Aye!" Grumpy nodded. "There's dirty work goin' on!"

"Sink's empty," called Sneezy from the other side of the room. "Someone's stolen our dishes!"

"They aren't stolen." Happy turned from the open cupboard. "They're all hid in here."

"Somethin's cookin'!" Sleepy sniffed the air, a smile spreading slowly over his droopy-eyed face.

The dwarfs gathered around the huge iron pot that was bubbling over the fire. Happy grabbed a spoon.

(22)

"Don't touch it!" warned Grumpy.
"It might be poison!"

Suddenly the pot hissed and bubbled.
The dwarfs jumped back in alarm.

"See—it's a witch's brew!"
cried Grumpy.

Some of Snow White's bird friends
had remained in the cottage when the
other animals had fled. From their
vantage point in the rafters, they
grinned down at the dwarfs. One
mischievous bird began tapping on the
wood with his beak.

"What is that?" Happy's
voice trembled, and his startled glance
darted from side to side.

"Sounds close!" Bashful glanced around fearfully.

One of the birds suddenly gave a scream, and the dwarfs all dove for cover. Sneezy jumped into an empty jar, Sleepy found a bucket, Happy cowered under a chair, and Dopey crawled under the woodpile. Grumpy hid in a potato sack, while Bashful braved the dark under the stairs.

"It's upstairs!" Doc was the first to speak. "One of us has to go down and chase it up, er, up…down."

Nobody volunteered. The dwarfs looked at each other, then turned toward Dopey and pointed.

Dopey shifted nervously from one foot to the other, looking up at the ceiling and down at the floor—anywhere but at the other dwarfs. He started to edge away, but before he could escape, the others rushed forward and caught him. Doc lit a candle and thrust it into Dopey's hand.

"Here," he whispered. "Take this. And don't be nervous!"

Six pair of hands pushed Dopey up the stairs. "We're right behind you!"

Dopey mounted the stairs reluctantly and reached the bedroom door. He pushed it open and edged his way inside, candle held out in front of him. At first he noticed nothing unusual.

Then Snow White yawned and stretched. Covered by a blanket as she was, she resembled nothing so much as a huge ghost. Dopey turned and fled, waving his arms wildly, and ran smack into the other dwarfs.

All seven dwarfs bumped and clattered down the stairs, landing in a heap at the bottom. Picking themselves up, they ran out the front door, slamming it on poor Dopey.

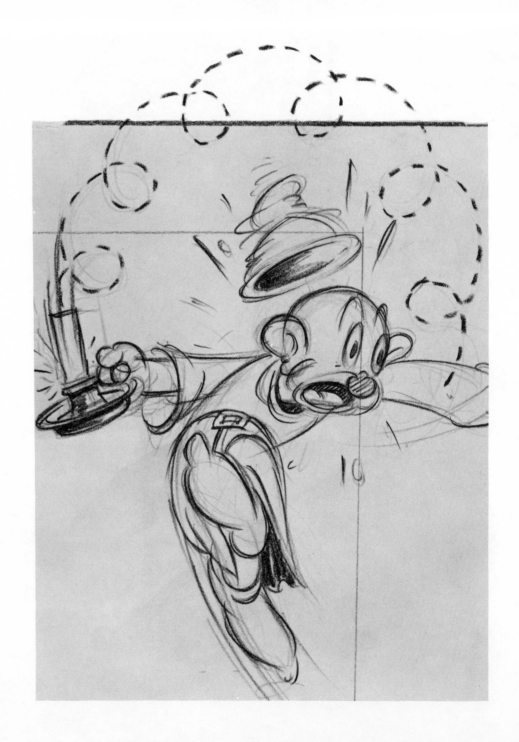

"Don't let it out!" yelled Happy. "Hold the door shut!"

Inside the cottage Dopey tugged frantically at the door. He could hear the "ghost" stirring upstairs. He yanked even harder, setting one foot against the doorjamb. All of a sudden, he found himself tumbling head over heels back across the room, into the cupboard where the pots and pans were kept. The cupboard door flew open and the pans tumbled out, one very large pot completely covering Dopey's head. The poor little dwarf rushed about in confusion, then found the door and pushed at it.

Then the front door swung open, and Dopey fled to the safety of the darkened clearing outside.

"Here it comes!" Happy whispered. "Now's our chance." For none of them knew Dopey in his saucepan-hat. And the dwarfs attacked the unfortunate Dopey, convinced that he was surely the "ghost."

"Hold on!" shouted Doc, as the "ghost" fell under a rain of blows and revealed Dopey's large, ungainly feet. "It's...it's Dopey!"

They dragged Dopey to his feet and crowded around him, firing questions.

"Did you see it?"

"Was it a dragon?"

"Did it breathe fire?"

Dopey gave an imitation of a slumbering beast. "He says it's a monster!" yelled Doc. "Asleep in our beds! Let's...attack!"

Their courage returning, the seven little men stole back into the cottage, ready to do battle with a fearsome monster. Holding their breath, they crept upstairs and pushed open the bedroom door. With Doc holding a lantern aloft, they slipped inside.

Snow White moaned softly in her sleep, and the dwarfs jumped back in alarm.

"What a monster!" hissed Doc. "Covers three beds! Let's get it before it wakes up!"

They moved forward again and stood looking down at Snow White's blanket-covered form.

As they raised their pickaxes to strike her, Snow White murmured in her sleep and turned over, and the dwarfs saw what the "monster" was.

"Why, it's a girl!" exclaimed Doc.

"Ain't she purty?" breathed Sneezy, fighting back a sneeze.

"Just like an angel," murmured Bashful, blushing.

"Huh!" Grumpy snorted. "She's a female, and all females is poison!"

Doc adjusted his spectacles. "Ssh!" he whispered. "You'll wake her up."

"Aw, let her wake up," replied Grumpy. "She don't belong in our beds, nohow!"

Snow White stirred again, and Bashful took a step backwards. "Look out! She's wakin' up!"

"Hide!" snapped Doc. "Quick!"

The dwarfs had just hidden behind the beds when Snow White sat up. She looked around and blinked in the lantern light.

"Ohh," she yawned. "I wonder if those children have returned yet."

The dwarfs exchanged puzzled glances. They didn't see any children.

Then the Princess noticed the seven pairs of eyes peering at her. She gave a little shriek and pulled the blanket over her head. The dwarfs ducked, too.

Soon everyone risked another peek.

"Why," said Snow White, "you're not children at all—you're little men! Well, how do you do?"

"How do you do what?" snorted Grumpy, folding his arms.

"Oh, you can talk!" said Snow White with a smile. "I'm so glad. Now, don't tell me your names—let me guess. You must be…" she paused, pointing at Doc. "You're Doc!"

"Why, yes!" answered Doc, his spectacles sliding down his nose. Then the Princess went on to match each of the other dwarfs with the names she'd seen carved on their little beds.

When she had finished, Grumpy was still unsatisfied. "You know who we are," he growled. "Now tell us who you are—and what you're doin' here!"

"How silly of me," Snow White replied. "I should have introduced myself. I'm Snow White."

"Snow White!" the dwarfs echoed. "The Princess?"

Snow White nodded.

Doc was impressed. "Well, well, my dear," he said. "We're mighty honored. We're…"

"Mad as hornets," put in Grumpy.

"Mad as hornets," repeated Doc. Then he realized what he'd said.

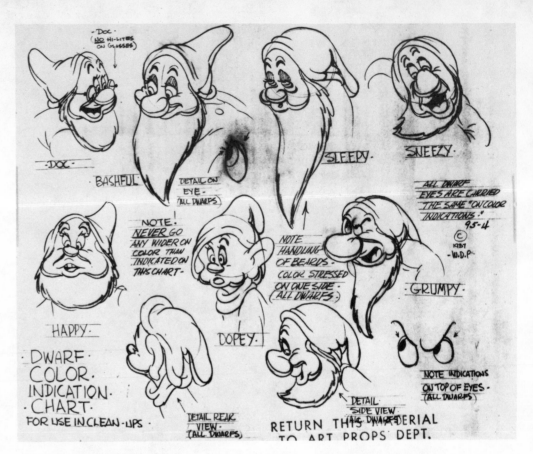

Doc frowned at Grumpy. "No, we're not, we're bad as cornets, er…no, no, bad as, uh…what was I saying?"

"Nothin'," muttered Grumpy. "You were just sputterin' like a doodle bug."

"Who's butterin' like a spoodle dug?" asked Doc indignantly.

"Aw, hush up," replied Grumpy, "an' tell her to git out!"

At his words, Snow White's smile disappeared, and tears began to fill her eyes. "Please don't send me away," she pleaded. "She'll kill me!"

"Who'll kill you?" asked Doc.

"My stepmother, the Queen!" the Princess replied, her eyes full of fear.

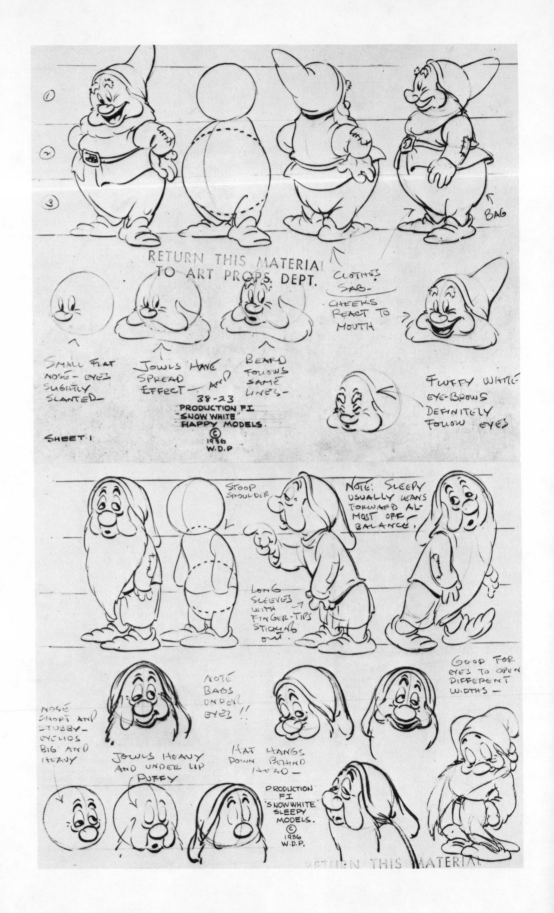

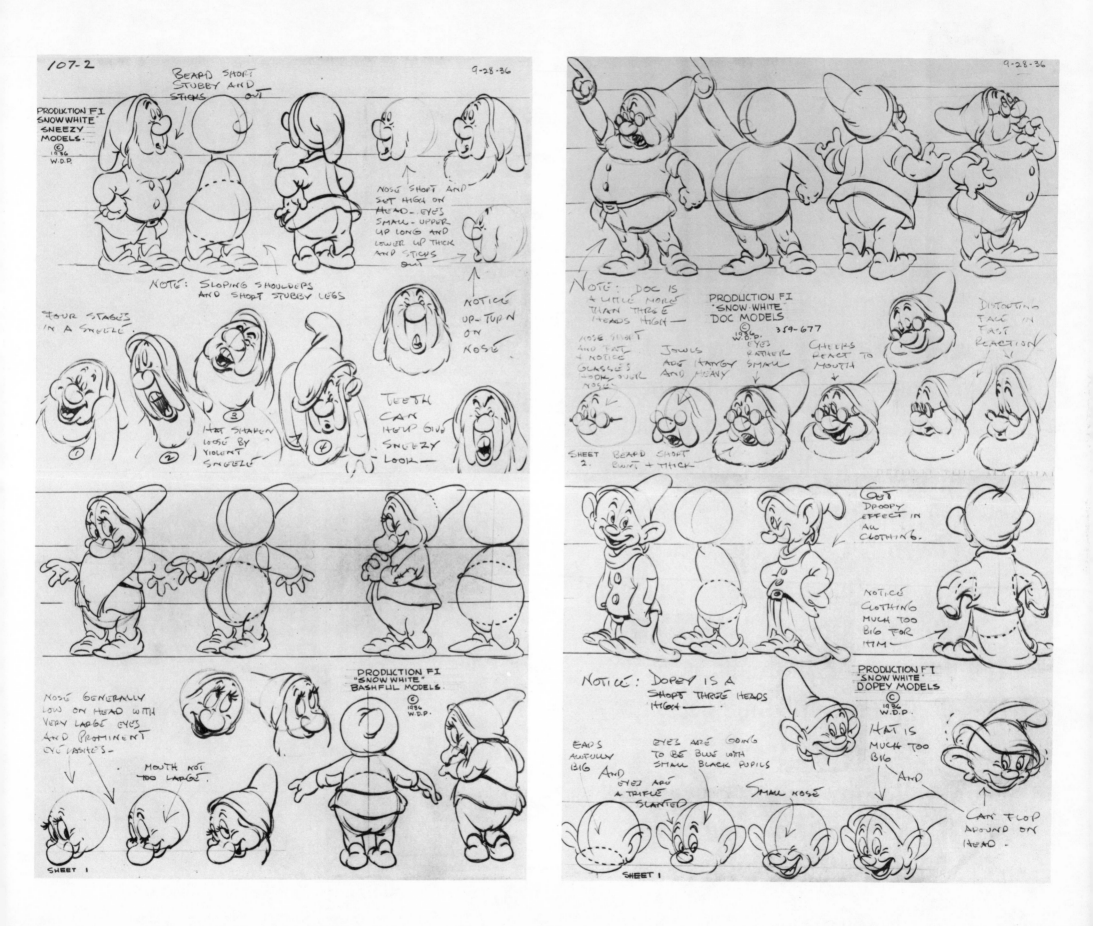

The dwarfs were shocked. "She's wicked!" said Bashful.

"A witch," Grumpy added. "And I'm warnin' you—if the Queen finds her here, she'll take it out on all of us!"

"But she doesn't know where I am," protested the Princess.

"Don't you bet on it," sneered Grumpy. "The Queen knows everything! She's fulla black magic!"

The dwarfs looked around nervously.

"Oh, she'll never find me here," Snow White assured them. "And if you'll let me stay, I'll keep house for you. I'll wash, and sew, and sweep, and cook..."

"Cook!" responded the little men with eager faces.

"Can you make dapple lumpkins?" Doc licked his lips. "I mean, apple dumplings?"

"Oh, yes," answered Snow White. "And plum pudding, and gooseberry pie, and tarts and…"

"Gooseberry pie!" Even Grumpy was impressed.

"Hooray!" cried the seven dwarfs. "She stays!"

Suddenly Snow White remembered. "The pot!" she cried, and jumped up. She rushed down the stairs, the dwarfs streaming after her.

hile Snow White tended to the cooking pot, the dwarfs scrambled into their places at the table. The Princess turned to them, spoon in hand. "Supper's almost ready," she announced. "You'll just have time to wash."

"Wash!" chorused the dwarfs, aghast at the idea.

"I knowed there was a catch," muttered Grumpy.

"Why wash?" Happy for once wasn't smiling.

"Tain't even New Year!" Doc pointed out. Even he was dismayed at Snow White's suggestion.

Snow White left the fireplace. "Let me see your hands." Seven pairs of hands immediately hid behind seven little backs, and seven little faces put on seven innocent expressions.

"Come on," she gently urged. "Let me see them."

Reluctantly each of the dwarfs held out his hands, and Snow White examined each one, her expression getting sterner with each inspection.

"This will never do," she declared, shaking a finger at them. "Now you all march straight out and wash, or you don't get a bite to eat!"

126

A very subdued group of little men filed out the door, except for Grumpy, who stood his ground and crossed his arms with an air of defiance.

Snow White turned to him. "Well," she demanded. "Aren't you going to wash, Grumpy?"

Grumpy refused to answer.

"Cat got your tongue?" she chided gently.

Abruptly Grumpy stuck out his tongue at her, turned on his heel, and stalked outside.

In front of the cottage the dwarfs were gathered nervously around a tub of water. "Courage, men," said Doc.

FEET OF
CHARACTER
SHOULD REG B
THESE LINE

He heartily rolled up his sleeves. "It'll please the Princess," he added.

"In that case," said Happy bravely, "I'll chance it!" And the others followed suit, with much splashing and sputtering. All except Grumpy.

"Her wiles are beginnin' to work," he remarked slyly. "I'm warnin' you—give women an inch, and they'll walk all over you."

"Don't listen to the old warthog," advised Doc, trying to pretend he liked the idea of washing up.

"Will our whiskers shrink?" Sleepy looked worried.

130

"Do you have to get in the tub?"
Happy was perplexed.

"You don't have to wash where it
doesn't show, do you?" Bashful was
reluctant to roll his sleeves up above
his elbows.

"Now, don't get excited," admonished
Doc. "Tain't no disgrace. Just roll up
your sleeves, take some soap, work up
a lather and rinse off."

Grumpy looked on in disgust as Doc
scrubbed all the dwarfs' bald heads.
"Next thing you know," he declared,
"she'll be tyin' your beards up in pink
ribbons. Huh! I'd like to see anybody
make me wash if I didn't want to!"

That was all the suggestion the others needed. They grabbed Grumpy, carried him over to the tub and immersed him in the water. Over his strenuous protests, that cantankerous dwarf found himself scrubbed clean as a whistle.

"You'll all pay for this!" he fumed, blowing soap bubbles.

"Supper!" Snow White called from the cottage.

"Food!" And they all rushed inside.

At the very moment the seven dwarfs were sitting down to a home-cooked meal, the wicked Queen was making her nightly visit to her Magic Mirror, in her hands the casket her huntsman had brought back from the woods.

134

Gazing into the mirror, the wicked Queen felt a strange sense of joy. This time, the mirror could give her only one answer.

"Magic Mirror on the wall," she chanted triumphantly. "Who is now the fairest one of all?"

A face emerged from the murky depths of the mirror. Its expression was one of contempt as it answered the Queen's question.

Over the seven jeweled hills,
Beyond the seventh fall,
In the cottage of the seven dwarfs
Dwells Snow White,
Fairest one of all!

The Queen was stricken. "Snow White lies dead in the forest!" she cried in disbelief. "I have proof! Behold—her heart!" And she opened the casket.

But the face in the mirror still mocked her. "'Tis the heart of a pig you hold in your hand."

The Queen looked down in dismay. "I've been tricked!"

The wicked Queen's rage was unleashed. Her cape swirling about her, she stalked from the room and down the stone steps to the depths of the castle. She entered a dank room and slammed the door behind her, startling a raven.

"The heart of a pig!" she snarled, her fists clenched at her side. "That blundering fool! I shall see to this matter myself!" And she took down an ancient book of spells and rapidly began to scan its pages.

"Ahh…" A sigh of satisfaction escaped her lips. "Just the disguise I need—a formula to transform my beauty into ugliness and my queenly gown—into a peddler's rags!"

Cackling with evil relish, she mixed her potion over a candle flame. "To shroud my clothes in the black of night," she chanted, as she dropped a pinch of blackness into the mixture.

"To age my voice, an old hag's cackle …a scream of fright to whiten my hair!" And a wisp of vapor took shape in the goblet and emitted a long-drawn ghostly shriek.

"A blast of wind to fan my hate," she continued, as a gust blew out the candle and plunged the room into darkness. "A thunderbolt to mix it with!" she screamed, and lightning flashed.

The raven stirred uneasily on its perch. Then the Queen regarded the potion. "Now begin thy magic spell," she rasped, and drank it down. Then she clutched at her throat.

the goblet crashed to the floor, and her figure became distorted. Everything seemed to spin around. The wicked Queen sank to her knees, clutching at her throat.

And the Queen's hair turned to white. Her hands became gnarled, and her voice a croak. In place of the haughty Queen stooped a bent-over crone.

"It is well," she hissed, and again began to turn the pages of the book of spells. "It shall be a special sort of death, for one so fair," she muttered. Then she found it.

"A poisoned apple!" she crowed. And she turned to her cauldron.

PRODUCTION FI
"SNOW WHITE"
WITCH MODELS.
FEB.25 1937   © 1937 W.D.P.   SHEET 1
1151-160

PRODUCTION FI
"SNOW WHITE"
WITCH MODELS
© 1937 W.D.P.
FEB.25 1937

SHEET 3
117-80

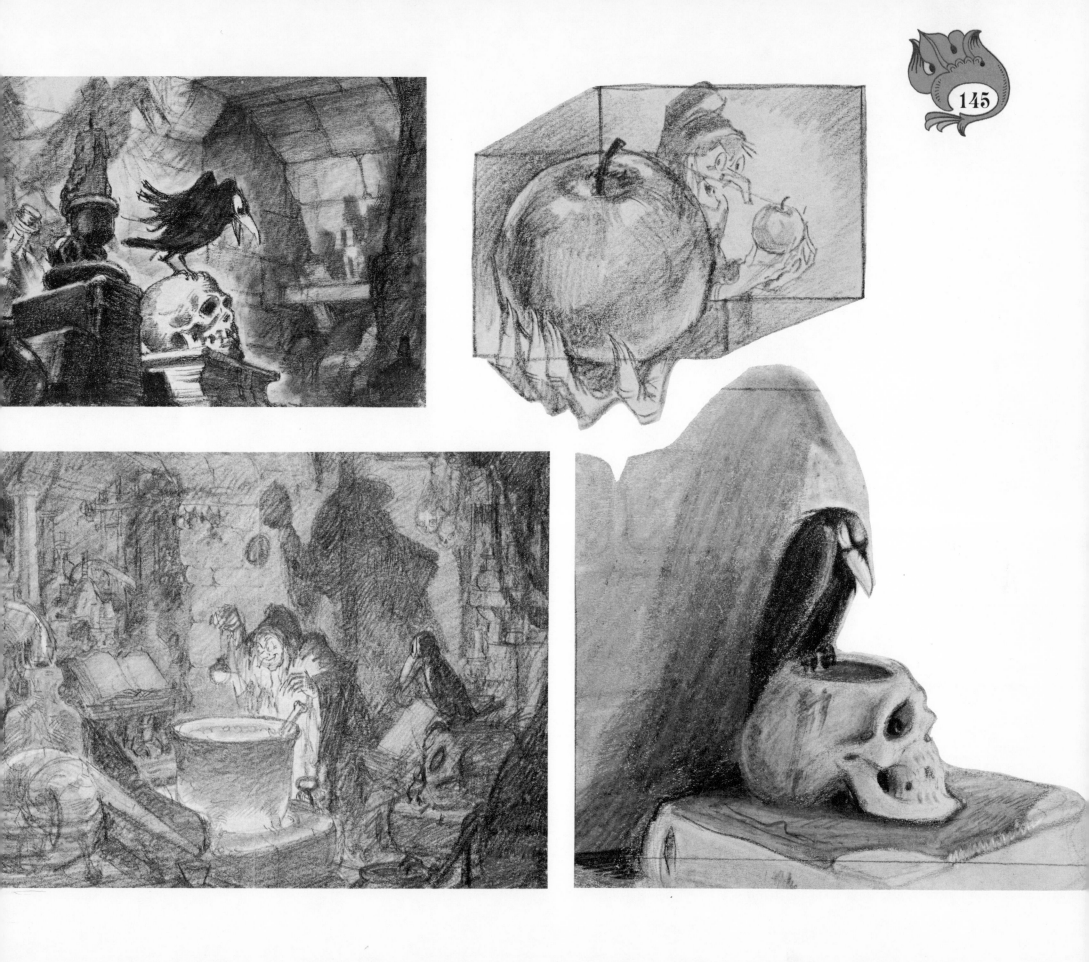

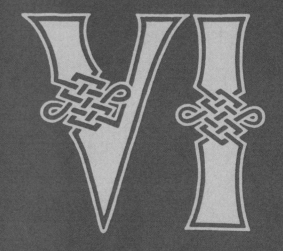

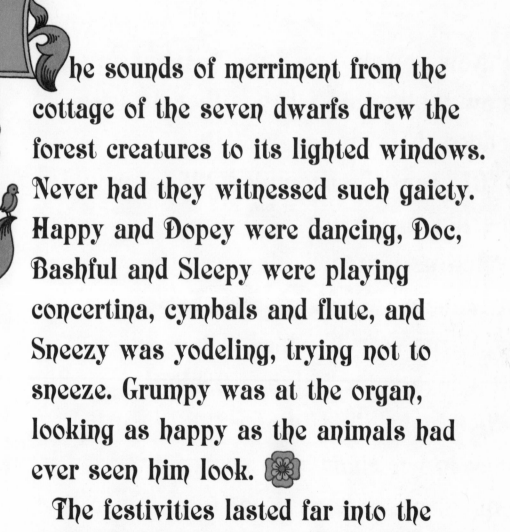

he sounds of merriment from the cottage of the seven dwarfs drew the forest creatures to its lighted windows. Never had they witnessed such gaiety. Happy and Dopey were dancing, Doc, Bashful and Sleepy were playing concertina, cymbals and flute, and Sneezy was yodeling, trying not to sneeze. Grumpy was at the organ, looking as happy as the animals had ever seen him look.

The festivities lasted far into the night, but finally Snow White and the dwarfs collapsed into their chairs, tired but happy.

"Oh, what fun!" breathed Snow White.

"Now you do somethin'," Happy urged Snow White, and all the other dwarfs nodded their approval.

"Of course," she smiled. "What would you like me to do?"

"Tell us a story!" clamored the little men.

"A true story!" added Doc.

"A love story," sighed Bashful.

"All right, then." Snow White settled back in her chair, and a wistful expression stole over her face. "Once there was a princess, who fell in love with a prince..."

"Was it hard to do?" asked Sneezy.

"Very easy," replied the Princess.

"Anyone could see the prince was charming—and the only one for me!"

"Was he strong and handsome?" asked Doc.

"Was he big and tall?" murmured Sleepy, blinking drowsily.

"There's no one like him anywhere," sighed Snow White.

"Did he say he loved you?" asked Bashful eagerly.

"Did he steal a kiss?" Happy grinned and winked.

Snow White looked off in reverie. "I just know I'll meet him again, and we'll be married and live happily ever after."

Just then the clock on the wall chimed. "Oh, my goodness!" exclaimed the Princess. "It's long past bedtime. Now go right upstairs to bed—every one of you!"

The dwarfs obediently headed for the staircase. Then Doc called a halt. "Hold on there, men! The Princess will sleep upstairs in our beds."

"But…where will you sleep?" asked Snow White.

"Oh, we'll…" Doc thought a moment. "We'll be quite comfortable down here in a…in a…"

"In a pig's eye," concluded Grumpy. Doc shot a frown at him.

155

"We'll be very comfortable down here, won't we, men?"

"Oh, yes," they chorused. "Mighty comfortable!"

"Now don't you worry about us," Doc smiled at Snow White. "You go right on upstairs."

"Well, if you insist…" The Princess went slowly toward the stairs. "Good night, then. And pleasant dreams."

The dwarfs settled down for the night in whatever sleeping places the cottage afforded—a drawer, a bench, the cupboard, the sink. Upstairs Snow White knelt at her bedside to say her prayers.

"Bless the seven little men who have been so kind to me, and…may my dreams come true. Amen. Oh," another thought occurred to her. "And please make Grumpy like me."

Downstairs Grumpy was muttering to himself as he tried to get comfortable in a large pot. "Huh! Wimmen!"

Back at the castle, the Queen, now turned into a witch, bent over a steaming cauldron in the dungeon. Dangling an apple on a string from her gnarled hand, she dipped the fruit in the boiling liquid, and muttered the spell: "Dip the apple in the brew, let the Sleeping Death seep through!"

22A

22B

and HAPPY asleep in cupboard.

23

24

Over and over she chanted this spell, her eyes gleaming in triumph at the thought of Snow White biting into this apple. Then she held the apple aloft, and the liquid that dripped down its sides gave it the look of a skull.

"Look, on the skin," she gloated, "the symbol of what lies within. Now turn red to tempt Snow White, and make her hunger for a bite!"

The apple began to glisten shiny red. The Witch's raven edged closer.

"Have a bite?" cackled the Witch, thrusting the apple at the raven. But it backed away as if it knew the fruit was poisoned.

"It's not for you, anyway," she leered, "but for Snow White! Once my rival tastes this apple, I'll be the fairest in the land!"

"But wait!" She turned back to the book of spells. "There may be an antidote! I must overlook nothing!" Her long crooked finger traced some fading lines.

"Aha!" she croaked. "Love's first kiss—no fear of that!" And she closed the book with a bang.

Laughing maniacally, the wicked Witch grabbed up a basket of apples, placed the poisoned fruit on top, and set out on her evil errand.

fter a delicious breakfast the next morning, the seven dwarfs set off for the mine. Snow White went to the door to see them off.

"Now, don't forget, Princess," cautioned Doc. "The Queen's a sly one, full o' witchcraft. So beware of strangers!"

"Don't worry," Snow White smiled, seeing his look of concern. "I'll be careful, I promise." And she lifted Doc's hat and gave him a kiss on top of his bald head.

"Well, come on, men," said Doc, blushing to the tips of his ears, "we've got a lot of work to do!"

Each of the dwarfs filed up to Snow White to repeat Doc's warning, and she kissed each one on top of his head, as she had Doc. Only Grumpy stood apart.

"Disgustin'!" he muttered.  "Everybody's goin' soft!" And when Snow White kissed him, too, on his bald pate, he made a great show of dignified indifference, hoping no one would notice how much he enjoyed it.

"Run along, then," waved the Princess, and she turned back into the sunlit cottage.

A few minutes later she heard footsteps. "Why, if it isn't Grumpy!" she exclaimed.

The cantankerous little dwarf walked in, hesitated, and looked about. "Now I'm warnin' you!" He paused to clear his throat. "Don't let nobody or nothin' in the house." And he stood there expectantly.

"Oh, Grumpy!" cried Snow White. "You do care about me!" And she bent down and gave him another kiss.

"Humph!" he grunted, and stalked out to join the other dwarfs. He was in such a hurry to catch up that he slipped on the bank of the stream and fell into the water. Sputtering, he hauled himself out of the stream, only to bump his head on the bridge.

Then, setting his face in his habitual scowl, Grumpy rushed off to the mine.

Not long after the dwarfs left for work, the wicked Witch arrived at the clearing. "With the little men away, she'll be alone," she congratulated herself. "She'll never suspect a harmless old peddler-woman." And she cackled softly.

Unaware of the menace lurking outside, the Princess Snow White hummed cheerfully as she trimmed pastry for the pies she was making for her seven little benefactors.

Suddenly a shadow fell across her, as she worked at the sunny window.

The animals scattered into hiding. "Oh!" she gasped. Although she had been startled, the Princess recovered quickly when she saw the old peddler-woman at the window.

"I'm sorry," she said, ashamed of herself for being so frightened. "You startled me."

"That's all right, dearie, I mean no harm," the Witch lied, resting her basket of apples on the window sill. "All alone, my pet?"

"Why, yes, I am," replied Snow White, seeing no reason to be suspicious.

"Mmmm, baking!" The crone's nose twitched at the fragrant smell.

"Oh, they do look delicious!" remarked Snow White, and she stretched out her hand.

"Go on, have a bite," the Witch invited.

The watching animals sensed that something was wrong. Snow White must not eat that apple!

"Makin' pies?"

"Yes," smiled Snow White. "Gooseberry pies for my friends when they return home from the mine."

"It's apple pies that make menfolk's mouths water," suggested the cunning Witch, holding out the lethal apple. "Pies made from apples like these!"

The birds swooped down on the old hag and knocked the apple out of her hand. Then they attacked her, and she flung up her arms to protect herself.

Snow White went to the old woman's defense. Beating at the birds with her hands, she drove them away. "Shame on you!" she scolded. "Shame on you, frightening a poor old lady!"

The birds retreated, and the Witch, down on her hands and knees, grabbed the fallen apple. Snow White helped her to her feet.

"I'm so sorry," she said, brushing dirt from the crone's rags.

"Oh! My heart!" cried the Witch slyly.

"Some water, please!" begged the crone.

Snow White, tender-hearted as always, helped the old woman back into the cottage. She slammed the door behind her to keep the forest creatures out, and gave the Witch a cup of water.

The birds and animals knew there was only one way to save Snow White now. And they set off at top speed for the diamond mine.

Inside the cottage, the old hag had made a remarkable recovery. "You've been so kind to old Granny," she wheezed. "I'd like to share a secret with you." She bent closer to the Princess, holding out the apple.

"This is a Wishing Apple!"

"A Wishing Apple?" said the Princess in wonder.

"Yesss," hissed the wicked Witch. "One bite, and all your dreams will come true!"

"Really?" Snow White took the apple the crone was pressing into her hand.

"Yes, girlie," leered the Witch. "All you have to do is make a wish and take a bite."

As the unsuspecting Snow White opened her mouth to take her first bite of the poisoned apple, she could already see her handsome Prince riding towards her.

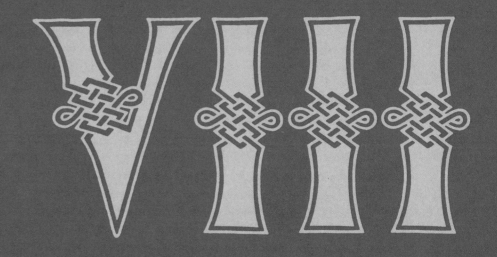

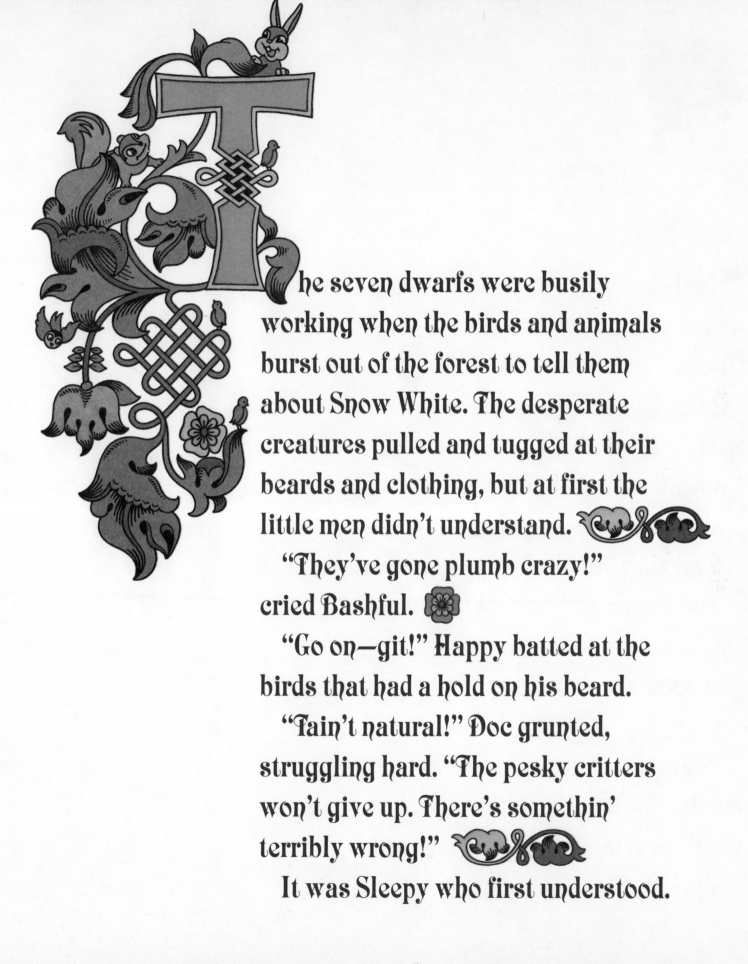

he seven dwarfs were busily working when the birds and animals burst out of the forest to tell them about Snow White. The desperate creatures pulled and tugged at their beards and clothing, but at first the little men didn't understand.

"They've gone plumb crazy!" cried Bashful.

"Go on—git!" Happy batted at the birds that had a hold on his beard.

"Tain't natural!" Doc grunted, struggling hard. "The pesky critters won't give up. There's somethin' terribly wrong!"

It was Sleepy who first understood.

186

"Maybe…" His voice failed him as the awful thought struck him. "Maybe the Queen's got Snow White!"

"The Queen!" gasped Doc. "That's what's up with these critters! The Queen'll kill her! We gotta get back—and quick!"

And they all sped off to the rescue.

The Princess Snow White was thinking about her handsome Prince as she took the first bite of the poisoned red apple.

"That's it," urged the Witch, rubbing her hands together. "Go on, go on—eat it all, dearie, and your wish will come true!"

"I feel so strange…" began Snow White, and she slumped to the floor, the half-eaten apple rolling out of her limp hand.

The Witch looked down at her in triumph. "Now," she cackled, "I will be the fairest in the land!" And again she laughed in mad glee.

She moved to the door, her mission completed. Outside a storm had come up. Lightning silhouetted the evil Witch's bent figure as she paused in the clearing. Over the crashes of thunder she heard other sounds—the shouts of the dwarfs and the drumming of running feet.

As the rescue party burst into the clearing, the Witch turned with surprising agility and fled into the dark forest.

"After her!" yelled Doc.

The hag's only avenue of escape led up a rocky slope. When she reached the top, she turned to face her pursuers, only then realizing that her path ended on a precipice.

"Trapped!" she gasped. "Those meddling little fools! What will I do now?" She looked around frantically. She saw two vultures peering down at her from a dead tree, and a lone boulder balanced on the edge of the crag.

"I'll fix you!" she crowed. "I'll crush your bones!" And she grabbed a stout branch and began to pry at the boulder to dislodge it.

The wicked Witch exerted all her strength, and the great rock began to move. The dwarfs saw what she was doing, and flattened themselves against the slope. Before the boulder began to move, a jagged bolt of lightning struck the ledge where Snow White's evil stepmother stood.

As the seven little men waited for the boulder to crash down on them, the ledge crumbled. With an agonized scream the wicked Witch fell.

Down she tumbled, into the rocky valley below. In the silence that followed, the only sound was the flapping of the vultures' wings as they circled down toward the Witch's lifeless form.

There was no rejoicing when the dwarfs returned to their cottage, for they found their Princess white and still, lying where she'd fallen.

When they couldn't revive her, they laid her on a bier with candles around her head, and knelt near her until morning.

So beautiful was Snow White, even in death, that her seven little friends couldn't bring themselves to bury her. Instead, they fashioned a coffin of gold and crystal and set it in a leafy glade, determined to keep a vigil at her side. 🌸

One day a stranger entered the dwarfs' clearing. He was handsome beyond description, and rode a pure white horse.

"Good day," he called to the dwarfs as he dismounted. "I am searching for a beautiful princess. Her name is Snow White, and I've been told she can be found at the house of the seven dwarfs.

An awkward silence followed.

"Well," asked the Prince, "does Snow White live here?"

"Snow White is dead." Doc hung his head. "The wicked Queen poisoned her with an apple."

The Prince was stricken with grief.

"Show me where she lies!" he pleaded.

So the dwarfs led him to the glade where Snow White's crystal coffin rested beneath a blanket of fallen pink and white petals.

The creatures of the forest were there gazing reverently at the Princess they had befriended.

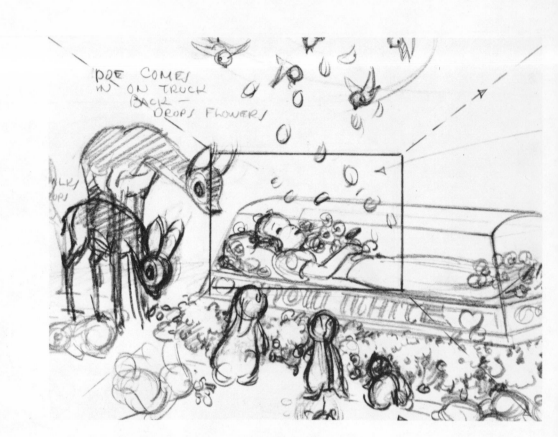

The dwarfs unfastened the transparent lid of the coffin and lifted it back, so the Prince could see that Snow White was indeed dead.

As he gazed at the Princess he'd searched for so long, the Prince bent down to kiss her.

"Tain't no use," murmured Doc.

The dwarfs knelt in a circle around the coffin, heads bowed.

But as they watched, Snow White began to stir, very faintly, as if awakening from a deep sleep. Her eyes opened and she smiled. As the animals and dwarfs looked on in disbelief, the Princess sat up and looked around. Then her gaze rested on the Prince.

"My Prince!" she murmured. "You've found me at last!"

"I've been searching so long!" he breathed, and kissed her again.

Rejoicing filled the air. The dwarfs danced for joy as the Prince lifted Snow White in his arms.

Suddenly Doc realized what was happening. "You...you're goin' away?" he asked, hat in hand.

For a moment Snow White's happiness was clouded by the thought of their sad parting. Then she smiled. "I am going away," she said. "But I shall never forget you!" And she kissed all her seven little friends on the tops of their dear, bald heads.

"Goodbye, Snow White!" They waved as they watched her ride off with her handsome Prince.

"Goodbye!" she called. The seven little dwarfs smiled after her—they knew she would live happily ever after.

Snow White and the Seven Dwarfs

THE END

About 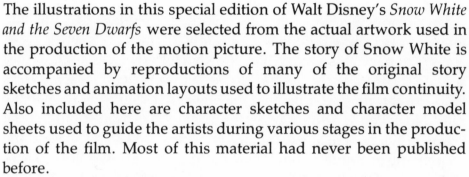 the Illustrations

The illustrations in this special edition of Walt Disney's *Snow White and the Seven Dwarfs* were selected from the actual artwork used in the production of the motion picture. The story of Snow White is accompanied by reproductions of many of the original story sketches and animation layouts used to illustrate the film continuity. Also included here are character sketches and character model sheets used to guide the artists during various stages in the production of the film. Most of this material had never been published before.

The production processes of the feature-length *Snow White* (begun in 1934 and continuing until the film's premiere in December 1937) were elaborations of the system developed by Walt Disney for the Mickey Mouse and Silly Symphony short cartoons which he had created previously; from story, story sketch, and layout, to animation, ink and paint, background, and recording, the procedure is still followed, almost exactly, in the production of all animated cartoons.

Story and story sketch are in a way synonymous, since the animated cartoon story artist illustrates the story with a series of sketches which delineate every phase of the action, dialogue, and camera moves. Sometimes he is aided by an artist specializing in character design, who makes more detailed drawings or portrays a mood or dramatic setting. On pages 12 and 14 of this book are examples of the refined, detailed story sketches which depict the action and establish the atmosphere for the opening scenes in *Snow White*.

Pages 27, 28, and 29 reproduce story sketches that were elaborately rendered to show Snow White's terror and confusion as she flees in panic through the forest after learning that the wicked

Queen planned to kill her. The completed sequence in the film follows very closely the mood and feeling of the story sketches.

On page 51 is a story sketch with a different function. Representing the front of the dwarfs' house in careful detail, it served as a guide for the artist who painted the finished background used in the film. No action is shown here; the rectangular frames outline the areas, or fields, which the camera photographed as it followed the movement of Snow White from the door to the window. These rectangular frames (called field guides), penciled on most of the story sketches, define the composition of each scene. Another example of camera field guides appears on page 71. Snow White has discovered the dwarfs' house and is examining their bedroom. The camera follows her point of view as she reads the names on the dwarfs' beds.

In contrast to story sketches, the purpose of which is to depict moods or backgrounds, are the sketches on page 64 which are deliberately simple and straightforward. They capture Dopey and Doc in a comic action with a minimum of background, so as not to distract attention from the action. Here, expression and characterization are the important elements in the scene.

The illustration on page 137 is an animation layout—it carries the story sketch process a step further, defining the setting and character action for production. Such layouts serve as guides for the animators; in this case, the layout indicates the path of action of the wicked Queen down the steps to her dungeon laboratory where she was to prepare the poisoned apple.

Pages 152 and 153 present another animation layout with a series of field guides to chart the movement of the camera panning across the dwarfs who are listening, enraptured, as Snow White tells a story. "Panning" is a term derived from "panorama," and is

used to describe the movement of a camera across a wide background area, such as a landscape or crowd, or from one subject to another when the distance between them is too great to be caught in a single shot.

Since consistency in the appearance of the characters is most important, especially with so many artists involved in the production, character model sheets, such as those shown on pages 112, 114 and 115, are prepared as aids to the animators. Here, the precise method for the drawing of each character is provided, along with suggested poses and attitudes that would suit their individual personalities.

The visual elements that make up an animated film reflect thousands of hours of work by hundreds of talented people. It was just such a cooperative effort, inspired and directed by Walt Disney, that made *Snow White and the Seven Dwarfs* a motion picture classic.

The Making of Snow White and the Seven Dwarfs

BY STEVE HULETT

When Walt Disney's first full-length animated feature, *Snow White and the Seven Dwarfs*, was released, the critics hailed it as a classic. But while the film was in production, Hollywood insiders referred to it as "Disney's Folly."

Walt's staff, of course, held a different view. They were dedicated and enthusiastic about the project, working long hours to see it through to completion. At the start, however, many of them were a trifle uneasy about embarking on something that had never been done before.

"One night early in 1935," says Disney veteran Ken Anderson, "we came back to the Studio to work after dinner, and Walt called forty of us onto the small recording stage. We all sat in folding chairs, the lights went down, and Walt spent the next four hours telling us the story of Snow White and the seven dwarfs. He didn't just tell the story, he acted out each character, and when he got to the end he told us that was going to be our first feature. We were overwhelmed.

"When Walt decided to do a cartoon feature it was a shock to all of us because we knew how hard it was to do a cartoon short. He was doing something no other studio had ever attempted, but his excitement over *Snow White* spread through the entire Studio."

The plot and dialogue for *Snow White and the Seven Dwarfs* were not simply the products of one late-night story session. Walt had been thinking about making a feature film for a long time. In many ways he had been moving toward it since the late twenties, when he first matched sound effects, music, and dialogue to a cartoon image in "Steamboat Willie." Strangely, *Snow White* was not the first feature-length cartoon contemplated by Walt. In the early thirties, when the Disney Studio was releasing shorts through United Artists, UA founder Mary Pickford had proposed a production of *Alice in Wonderland* with herself in the title role and the rest of the cast drawn by Walt's staff of artists.

"Mary was also going to put up all the money," Walt recalled years later. "I can still remember how awed we were when we figured that it would take four to five hundred thousand dollars to do a good job. It wouldn't have been too difficult to do in black and white, just a lot of intricate process shots, matching the animation to

the live-action figures. I worked out a plan, and we shot some test live-action footage. Then Paramount came along with a production of *Alice* and that knocked out our ideas."

Shortly after the *Alice in Wonderland* project fell through, Walt and Will Rogers discussed filming *Rip Van Winkle* with the little men done by the Studio animators, but Paramount wouldn't release its rights to the story, so nothing happened.

At the same time as these early feature ideas were falling through, Walt was making the two-dimensional world of the animated short more and more sophisticated. He added color. He refined the traditional boneless rubber-hose motion of his cartoon characters so that they moved more naturally and believably.

"I think Walt was always impatient with the restrictions of a cartoon," says Anderson. "He was constantly striving for more and more realism. I kept a notebook in those early days of camera angles and camera moves from live-action pictures. Walt took a look at the notebook and had others start keeping them too. He was always trying to overcome the limitations of the cartoon medium, though he never expressed it in so many words."

Walt Disney knew that *Snow White and the Seven Dwarfs* would require his staff of artists to draw and animate more naturalistically than ever before. "No one had ever animated a realistic girl," says Wolfgang Reitherman, longtime animation producer-director who was then an animator. "Cartoons had always been flat, with caricatures rather than real-looking people in them."

The Studio's first experiment with lifelike figures was in a 1934 "Silly Symphony" entitled "Goddess of Spring." Walt had used the Symphonies as a testing ground for new ideas and techniques since the ground-breaking "Skeleton Dance" in 1929. But this initial attempt to render human figures convincingly was a disaster.

"When the animators tried moving the goddess figure, the only thing they had to rely on was their experience with broad cartoon action," explains Wilfred Jackson, former animation director. "They'd never had to animate in a realistic way before, and the result was a goddess who moved stiffly and awkwardly. She was unconvincing as a human figure."

Walt wasn't discouraged. He went ahead with plans for a

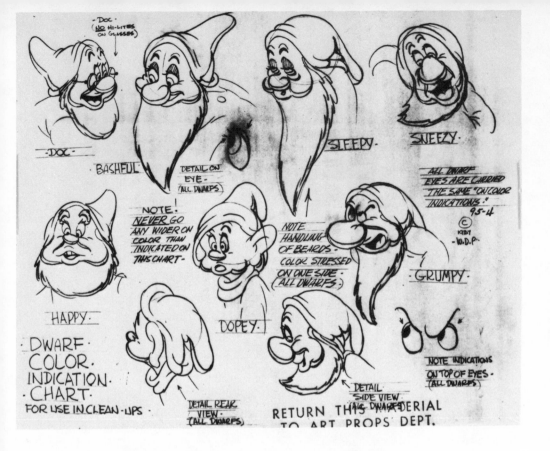

full-length feature, knowing it was almost an economic necessity. The introduction of double bills in movie theaters across the nation was pushing cartoon shorts off the screen.

Day by day Walt refined the story and the plot details. "He'd tell the story to anybody who'd listen," says Wilfred Jackson. "He'd tell it to an audience of two, four, or twenty. He'd pick the brains of animators, story men, and janitors, not always to get their ideas, but more to see how they'd react to a new twist he'd thought up. He'd watch their reaction and store it away in that marvelous brain of his, revise the story, and try it out again on somebody else. I don't think he ever forgot anything."

In mid-1935 Walt set up a small animation unit right next to his own office, where he put two of his top animators, Fred Moore and Vladimir Tytla, to work on test animation for the dwarfs.

"Fred was one of the most natural, intuitive animators that ever came through this place," says Woolie Reitherman. "He gave the dwarfs real appeal. And Bill Tytla was able to get a lot of power and weight into his animation, so they complemented each other well."

While the two of them worked, the story department wrestled with names and characters of the dwarfs. The Brothers Grimm had given the little men very little definition in the original tale, and it was up to Walt's story and gag men to flesh them out. Pinto Colvig, a story and voice man at the Studio (he was the voice of Goofy, as well as Sleepy and Grumpy) suggested giving each dwarf a name that would reflect a strong characteristic. From a long list that included Gabby, Jumpy, Sniffy, Lazy, Stubby, and Wheezy, the final seven were chosen. "Doc" seemed a good name for the leader of the dwarfs because it connoted someone in authority. "Happy" was a perfect counterbalance to "Grumpy." The names "Sleepy" and "Bashfull" lent themselves to endless gags. "Sneezy" was inspired by the actor who gave him voice—rotund Billy Gilbert had a trademark comedic sneeze.

Only "Dopey" posed a problem, not in his name so much as in his character. No voice for him pleased Walt, and dozens of artists tried and failed to capture his essence on paper. Then one night a story man attended a burlesque show and a round-faced little com-

edian named Eddie Collins came walking on. The story man took one look and knew he had found Dopey. The next day several members of the Studio staff brought Collins in for Walt to see, and it was unanimously agreed this was the perfect model for Dopey. The decision was made that, with such a baby-like face, Dopey needed no voice.

The next problem was finding suitable voices for the more realistic characters. Harry Stockwell was quickly chosen for the Prince, and Lucille LaVerne for the evil Queen. But finding a voice for the leading lady proved to be a major headache. More than a hundred and fifty girls auditioned for the part, identified only by number. Walt listened to them sing and speak from behind a screen, not wanting their physical appearance to influence his judgment. (One of the girls rejected was Deanna Durbin, just on the threshold of her career as a teen-age star at Universal. Walt decided that her voice, despite her youth, sounded too mature.)

Finally a girl named Adriana Caselotti, daughter of a well-known Los Angeles vocal coach, won the part. "All the dialogue and musical portions were done in a few days," she recalls, "but I felt very blessed. Not everyone gets the chance to introduce songs like 'Some Day My Prince Will Come' and 'Whistle While You Work.'"

By 1936, more and more of the Studio personnel were starting to work on *Snow White*. Walt had been preparing his staff for the assignment by having them attend drawing classes at nearby Chouinard Art Institute. And he had started hiring artists schooled in the fine arts of sculpture and painting. To be simply a cartoonist was no longer enough. Walt Disney needed actor-artists who could make each animated character a living, thinking personality in its own right. He assigned animators to the different characters as carefully as Jack Warner or Darryl F. Zanuck cast contract players for a live-action film.

A new animator, Frank Thomas, joined Fred Moore and Bill Tytla in animating the dwarfs. Eric Larson, Milt Kahl, and Jim Algar were given the task of bringing the forest animals to life. Norm Ferguson animated the witch. Ham Luske was put in charge of the film's leading lady.

"After the picture was done, I remember Walt saying that Ham really held the picture together with his animation," says Woolie Reitherman. "If Snow White hadn't been believable, I don't think the rest of the picture would have worked. One of the reasons why Ham was so successful was that he had great powers of analysis. He knew what poses to hit and to hold. I remember in a short called 'Elmer Elephant' he had the little elephant crying. He kept its head still and just had a tear slide down its trunk. It was very effective. With Snow White, even when he held her still he'd keep her dress moving to keep the animation alive. Snow White had a china-doll look to her, but in many ways I think she's the most successful girl we ever animated at the Studio."

Walt knew that if he was to get the realistic animation *Snow White and the Seven Dwarfs* needed, he had to work from realistic motion: live-action motion pictures. Actors, vaudeville performers, and Studio personnel danced, scowled, and hopped about in front of a movie camera, impersonating various characters in the film. For the complex sequence where Snow White enters the seven dwarfs' cottage for the first time, Ken Anderson built a scale model of its interior, one inch to the foot. He outlined it in black and photographed it with a close-up lens, panning from door to table. Next he shot a young female dancer named Marjorie Belcher (who later became Marge Champion of the famous Marge and Gower Champion dance team) as she pantomimed Snow White's entrance. Superimposing the two strips of film, Anderson created a lifelike guide for the animators and layout men to follow.

At that point, one of the *Snow White* layout men, a young Australian named Ken O'Connor, traced the live action off a Moviola onto animation paper one frame at a time, for there were no photographic frame blowups available in the mid-thirties.

"I'd impressed one of the directors with some of my drawing and the work over the Moviola was my reward," Ken recalls with a shudder. "I traced hundreds of frames of film every day for use by the animators. The only time I saw the sun was at lunchtime. I was getting downright sick of the job, but then one day Walt came in and told me how lucky I was to have this chance to study the way a

flesh-and-blood figure moved. The man could have sold an icebox to an Eskimo. By the time he left, his enthusiasm had got me looking at the job from a whole new perspective. I started tracing the live action with renewed enthusiasm."

O'Connor's tracings went to the animators, but they were used only as a loose guide. Proportions of figures were changed, and live-action timing was altered to get the movements the artists wanted. To follow O'Connor's work exactly would have made the animated versions stilted and unreal.

Live action wasn't much help where the dwarfs were concerned. There the animators were left to their own ingenuity to make Doc, Grumpy, and the rest totally separate entities.

"Animating the dwarfs represented the first time we'd ever had to delineate seven distinct individuals at one time," recalls Frank Thomas. "We'd animated lots of rabbits and mice in various scenes, but they were all pretty much indistinguishable from one another. In *Snow White*, if you had to do even a simple thing like backing the dwarfs up, you had to do each one differently. Now how many ways are there of backing up? You do the first four, and do them great, then you get to Sneezy and you've run out of ideas. And then there's Sleepy, and you have to do something with *him* that's different. It got to be a problem."

Walt's quest for perfection drove *Snow White*'s initial budget of half a million dollars higher and higher. He reviewed story boards, layouts, and preliminary backgrounds, looked at every foot of rough pencil animation. When something didn't please him he had no hesitation about having an artist redo it.

"We all had egos," recalls animator Eric Larson, "but Walt had a way of taking those egos and making them work together as a team. He had the ability to take you into a story meeting and tear a sequence or reel of animation apart and rebuild it so you had something concrete and solid. And he never forgot anything. If he said something to you it was a good idea to write it down, because he'd remember it even if you didn't."

If the animators found themselves being pushed to new levels of performance, they weren't alone. Every other department had to deliver things it had never delivered before.

Albert Hurter, a cigar-chewing Austrian who had been involved in animation since World War I (he had designed the houses, costumes, and principal characters for Disney's first big hit, "The Three Little Pigs") and Gustaf Tenggren, an award-winning illustrator of children's books, drew thousands of inspirational sketches for the film. They conceptualized the threatening forest into which Snow White escaped, rendered the gingerbread detailing of the dwarfs' house both inside and out, created the Witch's castle right down to the scrollwork around the leaded windows. Their sketches were passed on to art directors and layout men, who reinterpreted them in filmic terms, creating pleasing areas of light and shadow, staging each scene so that it not only was a work of art but provided characters with plenty of space in which to move.

"The biggest problem I always saw with putting together a long animated feature, with ten different art directors working on ten different sequences, was the difficulty of making the whole thing hang together," says Ken O'Connor. "You had people trying to outdo each other and you had to keep in mind the section of film that came after yours. And it was a good idea to know what came before. I found it remarkable that *Snow White* hung together as well as it did. But of course Walt had a good deal to do with that."

After layouts were completed (each the equivalent of a separate camera set-up in a live-action motion picture), they were given to the background department, which was facing new challenges of its own. "When I first came to the Studio," says O'Connor, "backgrounds were pretty meek and mild. Walt didn't want them to overpower the characters, so everything was in thin, watercolor washes." For the feature, the backgrounds were given a realistic solidity, but Walt wanted no bright, overpowering colors. He felt that strong color would be overwhelming for an hour and a half, so artist Samuel Armstrong came up with a muted palette of earth tones applied over stretched watercolor paper. That led to other problems:

"The animated characters were flat when painted on a cel," says O'Connor, "and they read flat against the more rounded backgrounds. In *Snow White* we tried to give the characters a rounded feeling to match the stronger backgrounds, and we got it by having

the ink-and-paint girls shade the edges of the characters with an airbrush."

One celebrated bit of production history is how the ink-and-paint girls gave Snow White's cheeks a rosy glow by rubbing real rouge on them. Walt was skeptical that it could be done believably until he saw the splendid results in the color dailies—the first film back from the lab.

To get the effects Walt wanted, Studio engineers and technicians developed a device called the multiplane camera. It was actually a sophisticated animation crane in which the far background, various middle distances, and foreground were placed at different levels in front of the camera lens. By moving the levels at different speeds and focusing on each level as characters reached them, the multiplane camera created the illusion that a character was moving in a three-dimensional world and not just between a sandwich of background and foreground plates.

The multiplane camera's only drawback was that it took a three-man crew days and sometimes weeks to photograph a scene, and if one step was bobbled on the last day of shooting, the whole complex scene could be ruined. But the huge expense the camera entailed didn't prevent Walt from saying enthusiastically to a *Time* magazine reporter, "It was always my ambition to own a swell camera, and now I've got one. I get a kick just watching the boys operating it, and remembering how I used to have to make 'em out of baling wire."

As he had with previous innovations, Walt first put the multiplane camera to use on a "Silly Symphony" to see what it could do. The result, an eight-minute short called "The Old Mill," won the Academy Award for best cartoon of 1937 as well as a special award for the creation of the camera.

With *Snow White*, even shooting the simpler scenes on the regular animation cameras was complex. After painted cels and backgrounds were photographed, the film had to be wound back and exposed again for shadow and light effects.

As the months went by and expenses continued to mount, the Studio was fast approaching the end of its financial rope. With credit over-extended, Walt and his brother Roy were facing over a

million dollars in expenses, but the worst was yet to come. Roy Disney informed Walt that they would have to borrow an additional quarter of a million to complete the picture. He told Walt that they would have to show Joseph Rosenberg of the Bank of America as much of the film as they had completed so far if they were to get a loan.

Walt reluctantly agreed, and on the appointed day he sat nervously in a projection room with Rosenberg, watching the color footage and pencil tests strung together in rough continuity.

"When it was over and the lights came on," Walt later recalled, "he didn't show the slightest reaction to what he'd just seen. He walked out of the projection room, remarked that it was a nice day, and yawned! Then he turned to me and said, 'Walt, that picture will make a pot full of money.' Well, we got the loan."

But to get *Snow White* completed for a Christmas 1937 release date was no longer just desirable; it was an absolute necessity. All Studio personnel were putting in fourteen- and sixteen-hour days, six and sometimes seven days a week. Their only incentive was enthusiasm for the new kind of film they were making and faith in Walt. "For months about all we did was wake up and go to the Studio, work all day and go home to bed," remembers veteran animator Ollie Johnston, who worked as an assistant to Fred Moore. "Studio wives got together for company. They were 'Disney widows' the way some wives today are golf or football widows. But they were all very supportive of what their husbands were doing."

As the film neared completion, Walt was forced to cut two sequences: one in which the dwarfs eat soup, and another where they build a bed for Snow White. Although entertaining, neither sequence moved the story forward, and they would have made the film far too long. Hundreds of feet of animation, both full and partial, representing thousands of hours of painstaking work, had to be left on the cutting-room floor. (None of them was destroyed, however; twenty years later, the completed animation for the soup-eating sequence was shown on Disney's television program.)

At last, in the first week of December 1937, a preliminarily "answer print" of the completed picture came back from the Technicolor laboratories. Walt loaded the film and fifty of his key

employees onto a bus and drove out to Pomona for a sneak preview.

"That preview was unsettling," says Wilfred Jackson. "The audience seemed to be enjoying the film, laughing, applauding. But about three quarters of the way through, one third of them got up and walked out. Everybody else kept responding enthusiastically to *Snow White* right to the end, but we were concerned about that third. Later we found out they were local college students who had to get back for their ten-o'clock dormitory curfew."

Snow White and the Seven Dwarfs had its world premiere at the Carthay Circle Theater in Los Angeles on December 21, 1937. The Christmas deadline had been met, but just barely. Walt had wanted the film to open in December coast to coast, but not enough prints could be made in time. In fact, the only two complete prints of the film were at the Carthay Circle Theater for the premiere, and Ken Anderson remembers that they arrived only a few hours before show time.

For many of the Disney staff, the premiere they attended was the first time they'd seen the entire production. "When we were making it," says Ollie Johnston, "we only got to see the sequences we were working on. When I wanted to see some of the others, somebody would tip me off they were screening them and I'd sneak into the projection booth down the hall to watch.

"I was plenty nervous when *Snow White* started that night at the Carthay Circle. All I could see was the mistakes in our animation. That opening sequence had been one of the first ones completed. But the audience was caught up by Snow White and the birds right away, and I relaxed."

"In the year and a half we worked on the picture," adds Frank Thomas, "the advances in animation were phenomenal. Some of the first animation of the girl has never looked good to me. Her eyes squeegee all over her face . . . she moves badly. But by the time we did the last stuff, for instance the scene where she's baking the pie at the dwarfs' cottage, the animation's great."

Fortunately, the opening-night audience of celebrities wasn't as hypercritical as *Snow White*'s animators. They laughed and applauded during the entire screening.

"They even applauded backgrounds and layouts when no

animation was on the screen," says Ken O'Connor. "I was sitting near John Barrymore when the shot of the queen's castle above the mist came on, with the queen poling across the marsh in a little boat. He was bouncing up and down in his seat, he was so excited. Barrymore was an artist as well as an actor, and he knew the kind of work that went into something like that."

The general public and film reviewers were as enthusiastic as the audience at the premiere. Over twenty million people went to see the picture on its initial release, and box-office records were shattered. *Snow White* rose to top *Variety*'s list of "All-Time Box Office Champs." *Time* magazine called the film "as exciting as a western, as funny as a haywire comedy . . . an authentic masterpiece." Frank Nugent in *The New York Times* declared, "If you miss *Snow White and the Seven Dwarfs*, you'll be missing the ten best pictures of 1938." The Metropolitan Museum of Art even asked for cels from the picture, in particular the two vultures animated by Ward Kimball. It was the first time any museum had asked for artwork from the studio of a "cartoon maker."

If Walt Disney was affected by all the praise, he did not show it. "Walt never had time to take bows or rest on his laurels," says Wilfred Jackson. "By the time a feature came out he was always in the middle of the next one."

Snow White's success made Walt determined not to lose any of the seven hundred and fifty artists who had worked to make it. The profits from the film meant he could build a new studio to house his growing staff and embark on an ambitious program of full-length animated films.

The enormous success of the world's first animated feature was just one more proof that, as *Time* magazine said, thirty-six-year-old cartoon maker Walt Disney was "no more a cartoonist than Whistler."

WALT DISNEY

❀ Presents ❀

Snow White
and the Seven Dwarfs

ADAPTED FROM
Grimm's Fairy Tales

SUPERVISING DIRECTOR
David Hand

SEQUENCE DIRECTORS
Perce Pearce
Larry Morey
William Cottrell
Wilfred Jackson
Ben Sharpsteen

SUPERVISING ANIMATORS
Hamilton Luske
Vladimir Tytla
Fred Moore
Norman Ferguson

STORY ADAPTATION
Ted Sears
Otto Englander
Earl Hurd
Dorothy Ann Blank
Richard Creedon
Dick Rickard
Merrill De Maris
Webb Smith

Snow White and the Seven Dwarfs

*The works of art reproduced in this book are over four hundred of the original
drawings, sketches, and paintings used for concept and design in the preparation of
Walt Disney's 1937 film,* Snow White and The Seven Dwarfs, *and preserved in
the archives of Walt Disney Studios.*

*Vladimir Yevtikhiev designed and executed the illuminations in the text. The
printing in four colors was by Federated Lithographers, Providence, Rhode Island,
and the book was bound by A. Horowitz & Son, Fairfield, New Jersey.
The endpapers are Multicolor, by Process Materials, Inc.
The cover material is Holliston's Lexotone.*

CHARACTER DESIGNERS
Albert Hurter
Joe Grant

BACKGROUNDS
Samuel Armstrong
Mique Nelson
Merle Cox
Claude Coats
Phil Dike
Ray Lockrem
Maurice Noble

VOICE TALENTS

Adriana Caselotti .... *Snow White*
Harry Stockwell .... *Prince Charming*
Lucille LaVerne .... *The Queen*
Moroni Olsen .... *Magic Mirror*
Billy Gilbert .... *Sneezy*
Pinto Colvig .... *Sleepy and Grumpy*
Otis Harlan .... *Happy*
Scotty Mattraw .... *Bashful*
Roy Atwell .... *Doc*

ANIMATORS

Frank Thomas	Les Clark
Dick Lundy	Fred Spencer
Arthur Babbitt	Bill Roberts
Eric Larson	Bernard Garbutt
Milton Kahl	Grim Natwick
Robert Stokes	Jack Campbell
James Algar	Marvin Woodward
Al Eugster	James Culhane
Cy Young	Stan Quakenbush
Joshua Meador	Ward Kimball
Ugo D'Orsi	Wolfgang Reitherman
George Rowley	Robert Martsch

MUSIC
Frank Churchill
Leigh Harline
Paul Smith

ART DIRECTORS

Charles Philippi	Tom Codrick
Hugh Hennesy	Gustaf Tenggren
Terrell Stapp	Kenneth Anderson
McLaren Stewart	Kendall O'Connor
Harold Miles	Hazel Sewell

Technicolor (R) Re-released by: Buena Vista Distribution Co., Inc.

Running Time: 1 hr., 23 min.